The Thief of Bracken Farm

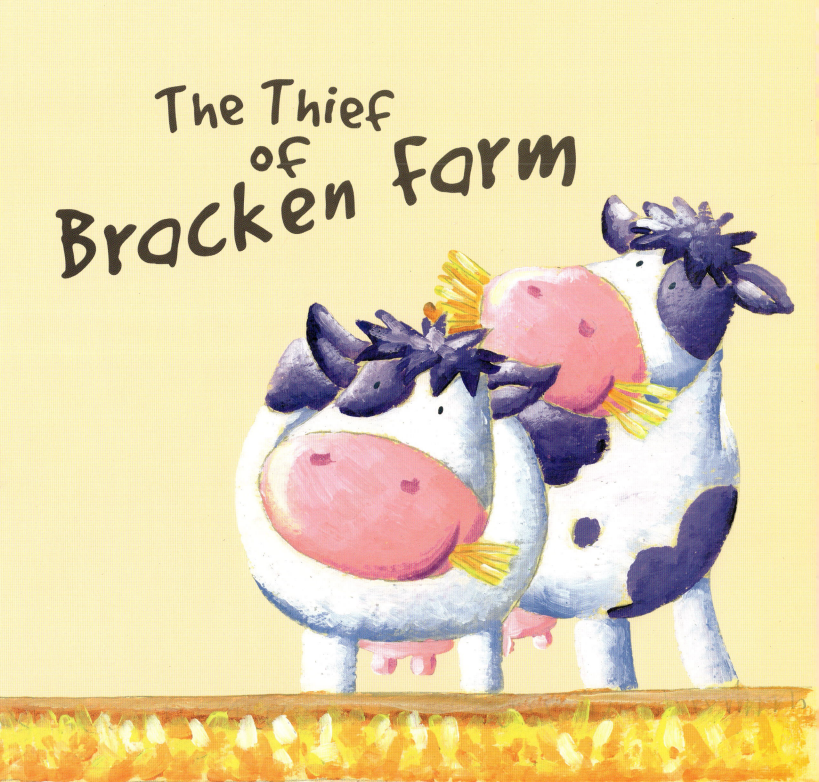

Library of Congress Control Number: 2006038312

ISBN 978-1-59566-338-2

Written by Emma Barnes
Edited by Clare Weaver
Designed by Susi Martin
Illustrated by Hannah Wood
Consultancy by Anne Faundez

Publisher Steve Evans
Creative Director Zeta Davies
Senior Editor Hannah Ray

Printed and bound in China

The Thief of Bracken Farm

Emma Barnes

Illustrated by
Hannah Wood

QEB Publishing

QEB

Some very strange things were happening at Bracken Farm.

"Where is my hat?" asked Farmer Jones.

"It's on your head!" shouted Ted and Bess.

Farmer Jones was always losing his hat. And it was always on his head.

"No, it's not," said Farmer Jones.
It was true. This time the hat was not there.

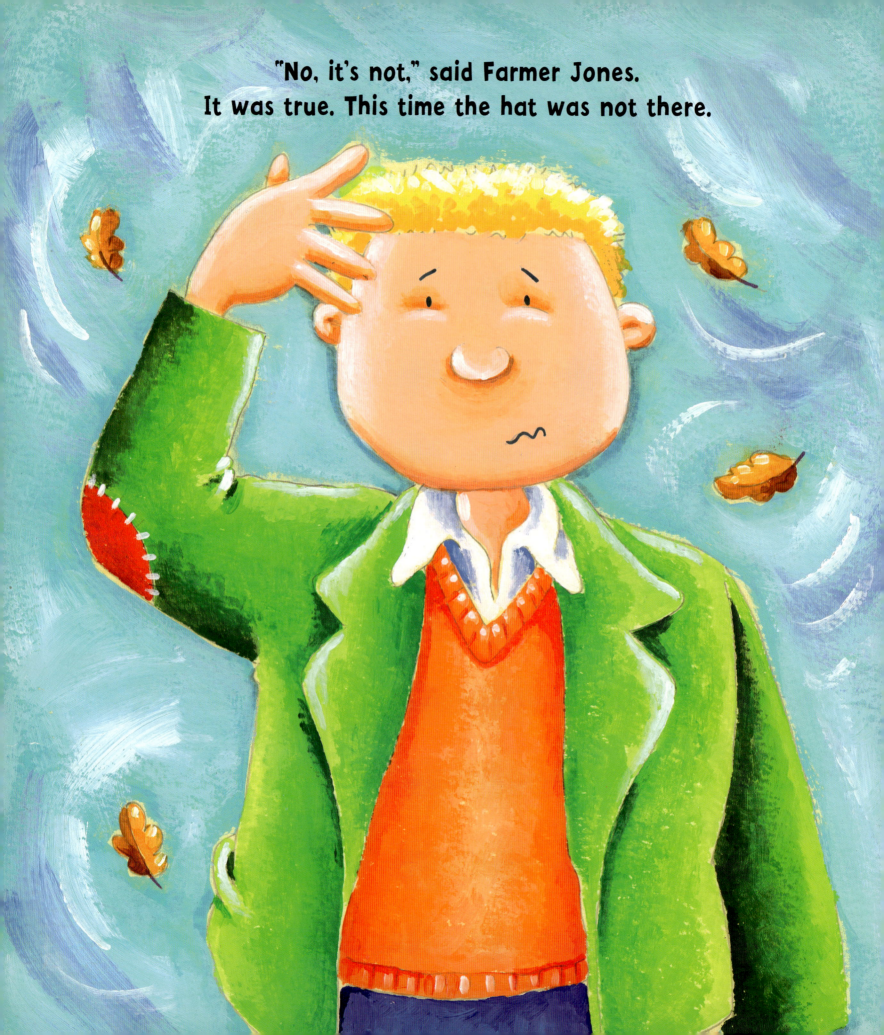

"In the tractor!"
shouted the children.

But the hat was
not there.

"In the barn!" they yelled.

But the hat was not there.

"We'll look for it," the children said. They went to the farmhouse. But they couldn't find the hat anywhere.

When they looked around, they noticed that many others things were missing, too.

Mrs. Jones had lost her scarf. The baby had lost her mittens. Marmalade the cat's blanket was not in her basket. And Ted couldn't find his homework anywhere!

"Poor Marmalade!" said Bess.
"She'll be cold without her blanket."

"Never mind that," said Ted.
"I'll be in big trouble without my homework. I think there's a thief!"

"A thief?" asked Bess.
"Why would a thief want your homework? I think there's a ghost!"

There was no point in arguing.
They started to look for clues.

First, they went to the orchard.
They saw many apples and pears,
but no thief.

Next, they went to the fields. They saw Adam the shepherd, Nell the sheepdog, and **54** woolly sheep...

but no thief.

Then they went to the farmyard. They saw hens, ducks, Tansy the goat, and...

There was somebody in Tansy's pen!
"I think the thief is stealing Tansy,"
Ted whispered.

The two children
crept closer. **And closer.**

They were standing right
next to the pen.

"STOP THIEF!"
they shouted.

The thief fell over. Only it wasn't a thief.
It was Miss Sanders the vet.
"You scared me!" she said.

The children explained that they were
looking for the thief of Bracken Farm.

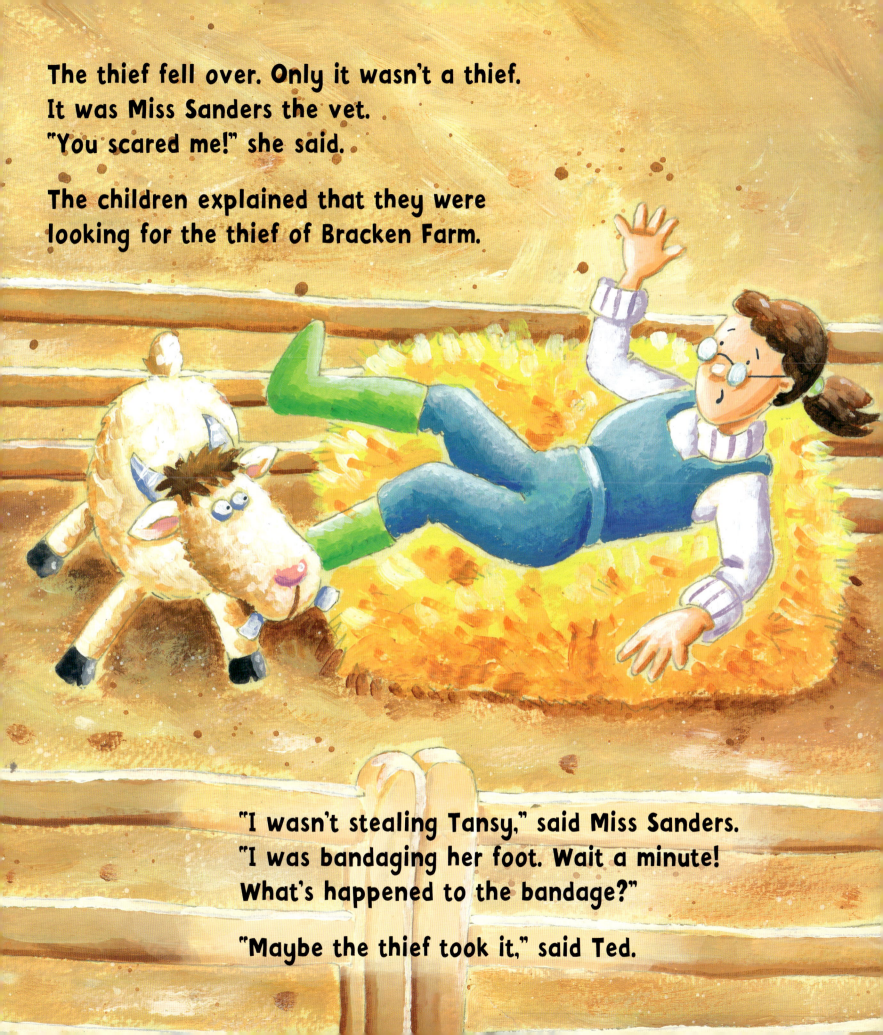

"I wasn't stealing Tansy," said Miss Sanders.
"I was bandaging her foot. Wait a minute!
What's happened to the bandage?"

"Maybe the thief took it," said Ted.

But the thief hadn't taken it. Tansy was eating it!

"Maybe Tansy ate the other things, too," said Bess. "Goats will eat anything."

Miss Sanders didn't think so. She told them that if Tansy had eaten a hat, a scarf, mittens, the cat's blanket, and Ted's homework, she would have a sick tummy, not a hurt foot.

Just then, they heard a shout from the stables. They went to see what had happened.

"It's Marmalade!" said Mrs. Jones. "It's time for her lunch. I've looked everywhere. She's gone!"

"Oh no!" said Ted. "The thief took Marmalade!"

They were all very sad. Nobody cared about Mr. Jones's hat, Ted's homework, or any of the other things. They all loved Marmalade the cat.

They were so sad that they were very, very quiet. And because they were so quiet, they heard a strange noise.

"Meooooooowww!"

"I told you there was
a ghost!" said Bess.

Ted went over to the cupboard.
He opened the door...

There was Marmalade! She had made a nest. She had used the hat, the scarf, the mittens, her blanket, and Ted's homework.

She also had four new kittens!

Notes for Teachers and Parents

- When you read the book aloud, enjoy the story, the humor, the excitement of what will happen next, and the rhythm of the words. Build up the suspense.

- Play a guessing game with the children. Who is the thief? What else might be missing? Let the children take turns reading the story aloud. Help them with difficult words. Remember to praise the children for their efforts.

- Discussing the characters and story afterward helps maintain interest and consolidates knowledge. Who is the children's favorite character? What is their favorite animal? Was it a big surprise that Marmalade was the thief? Or were there clues early on?

- Play a memory game with the children. Collect the objects that went missing in the story—a hat, mittens, a scarf, a blanket, and homework. Ask the children to study the objects for one minute. Then cover the objects with a cloth. How many objects can the children remember?

- Have the children make lists of the objects, learning to spell each word. Make a poster showing all the objects with the word written next to each picture.

- Encourage the children to create their own story about a thieving animal. What would go missing on the farm if a sheep were the thief? What things might a sheep take from the room the children are in? Or from the school playground?

- This story also lends itself to group artwork, such as a collage. Encourage the children to make separate drawings or paintings of the cat, each kitten, and all of the missing objects. These can then be mounted together on a large piece of paper. Pieces of wool and shredded paper can be glued onto the page to make a group collage.

- Help the children make a display of the farm itself, with a tractor, farmhouse, and all the different characters and animals. Incorporate many different materials: wool for the sheep, foil for the tractor, felt, cloth, leaves, twigs, etc. Another approach is to cut out pictures of animals from magazines to be glued onto the display. Words can be added to the picture, identifying the animals and the sounds they make, to encourage word recognition.

- Hiding places appeal to children. Encourage them to imagine they have a secret hiding place. Where would it be? In a cupboard or hollow tree? A cave? An attic? What would they keep there? What would they eat? Would they have a companion, such as a pet, a wild animal, or a toy? Come up with words to describe the den, such as spooky, cozy, dark, or secret. Let the children draw a picture of their imaginary den.